# TRAPPED

## IN THE TUTORIAL

## ANNA KOPP

ISBN: 1533174873
ISBN-13: 978-1533174871

# CONTENTS

# CHAPTER 1: TRAPPED!

P<small>OP! CRACKLE! POP!</small>

Red opened his eyes and jolted up at the sound of the explosion. At first, he thought he was still dreaming because the place he woke up in wasn't his bed. He looked around and realized that it also wasn't his house. It wasn't *any* house! Red was in the middle of a strange forest biome, and it definitely wasn't a dream.

How did he get there? The last thing he remembered was going to sleep in his comfy bed after a long day exploring. Red was an adventurer, and he loved discovering new places and searching for treasure. He had a home in the jungle biome, where he learned his survival skills. Still, even with all his experience, Red was worried. What happened to him?

The day was just beginning so Red decided to take a look around. It was grassy with lots of oak trees, and he spotted some water too. He could also hear a pig oink in the distance. Good, Red thought, lots of natural resources. This was definitely a lucky spawn. He came to a small clearing with an unfinished structure made from oak planks. It looked oddly familiar, like he'd seen it before. Next to it was a wooden sign. Red walked up to it and read 'Chop down four blocks of wood'. How strange, he thought, but decided to continue on.

Behind the clearing was a large chisel stone gateway with a narrow staircase. Red could see a fountain on the other side and a castle gleaming in the distance. He couldn't wait to check it out and hurried through.

BOINK!

"Ouch!" Red cried, as his face hit an invisible wall. He rubbed his sore nose and tried again, but slower this time. Nope! Something prevented him from going in. It was impossible. Confused, Red looked it over and noticed a sign on the side pillar. It read, 'You cannot leave this area until you have completed the Tutorial'.

"Aha!" Red realized. So that's where he was! The Tutorial was a special biome for new adventurers. It taught the basics of how to survive in the Overworld, like crafting tools and building shelter. Red had gone through it many years ago, which must have been why this place looked so familiar. So why was he there now? It made no sense!

Oh well, Red thought, no big deal. He would just have to complete it again so he could go home. There was no other choice. The starting area was surrounded by an impenetrable wall. He had no way to leave, so Red walked back to the sign with the first instruction. Four blocks of wood? No problem.

There were many trees and Red opened his inventory to take out the diamond pickaxe he made just yesterday.

"Oh no!" Red cried, "my stuff!" His inventory was completely empty! That meant his diamond tools, armor, potions, and other useful materials he kept on hand were all gone. Red felt both angry and upset, wishing this was all just a bad dream. But it wasn't. With a heavy sigh he decided it was better to continue his mission than sit there and feel sorry for himself.

Coming up to a tree, Red punched it with great force until it disintegrated into a block of wood. It made him feel a little better, and he continued on until four blocks appeared in his inventory. He walked back to the sign and saw that new words were written on it! Now it said 'Craft wood planks'. Easy-peasy, he thought, and created four planks from a wooden block.

The next mission said 'Eat to restore food bars and health'. Red realized just how hungry he was. Both his food bar and health level were depleted below half! If it dipped any lower, he would have no energy to walk or fight. He had to conserve his strength.

Red saw a pig, but decided to try and find some apples instead. He didn't know how long he would be stuck there and the pig was his only companion. He began breaking leaves off the oak trees in hopes of them dropping an apple.

BONK!

An apple fell right on his head! Red almost kicked it away in revenge but he knew the faster he ate, the faster his next mission would come. He gobbled up the apple but it wasn't enough, so Red continued his search. One tree was particularly leafy, so he aimed his sights and struck with all his might.

"AAAH!" Apples showered down on top of him. Red ducked out of the way, not wanting to get hit again. He'd never seen that before! Usually it took time and patience to find apples. He ate until his food bar was finally full and put the rest in his inventory just in case.

Next was one of the most important steps of all: creating a crafting table. Good thing Red already knew how to do that and put it in the clearing. He crafted some sticks, a shovel, and a pickaxe. Now that he had tools, he could mine stone. Red mined eight cobblestones and built a furnace to make charcoal. Everything was going smoothly and Red was hopeful he would be done soon.

The sign said he needed to make some glass and he ventured toward the water he saw earlier. It was just a small pond surrounded by sand. Red came closer and got his axe ready for mining. Except the yellow blocks were strangely smooth, and Red realized that it wasn't sand at all – it was sandstone! He walked around the entire pond, looking for sand, but it was nowhere to be found. He even tried to mine under the sandstone, and ended up splashing knee deep in water.

What now? If he couldn't get sand, he couldn't make glass, and without glass he couldn't complete the Tutorial. He could have sworn the last time there was no sandstone at all, so why was it there now? Mulling over the questions, Red headed back to the sign to see if maybe he could find some clues to help him.

POP! BANG! CRACKLE!

Red jumped with alarm and looked around in fright. His heart beat so fast he thought it would explode! Beyond the impassable gateway he saw sparks disappearing into the air. They were just fireworks! Red felt foolish for being scared of fireworks, but at least there was no one there to see his reaction.

When he finally reached the instruction sign, there was no change. It was still waiting for him to craft glass. He looked high and low, but found no tan blocks anywhere.

WOOOOSH!

Rain came out of nowhere! It fell so hard Red could hardly see anything in front of him. Completely soaked and with nowhere to wait out the rain, he began to mine the side of the wall. Luckily, he was able to get a few blocks in before the invisible force stopped him. It was enough to keep dry. Thunder boomed and lightning lit up the sky, but Red wasn't afraid. In the jungle, this was a regular occurrence. Red missed his home, and that made him even more determined to figure out a way to leave this place.

When the rain finally ended, Red noticed something different about the world. The sky was darker than usual. Oh no, Red realized, fear quickly growing inside him, it was almost nighttime!

# CHAPTER 2: THE FIRST NIGHT

Night? That's impossible, Red thought. In the Tutorial, time did not start passing until it was completed to give adventurers a chance to learn their new skills. However, he could not deny that there was something off about this particular place.

The sun was setting fast and Red had no shelter. He knew that hostile mobs would appear without light. Good thing he had some charcoal and sticks to make torches. That way he could at least make it so they didn't spawn right on top of him. Should he make a run for the half-finished structure and try to complete it or try and spend the night in the shallow cavern?

The distant moaning of what he knew were zombies answered that question. Red quickly began to build a wall, but soon realized he had no crafting table to make a door! He would have to venture out into the night if he wanted to survive.

Gripping his pickaxe, Red stepped out of his cave and looked around. He knew zombies had a habit of creeping up on people, and the last thing he wanted to be was zombie chow. He slowly moved toward the direction of the clearing. Even though it was dark, the torches from the gate were burning bright. Red was almost there when –

"BUUUH!" The low growl of the zombie was right behind him! Red turned around and swung his pickaxe. The green headed monster fell back, but not for long. It lunged at Red, trying to take him down. Red hit it over and over until it was finally destroyed. He was glad of his victory, but knew that if he didn't get to shelter soon, he would have to fight more mobs.

Finally Red reached the crafting table and furnace. He made some doors, a stone sword, and more charcoal for torches. Too bad he couldn't make a bed, he thought. That would make night much easier. He could just sleep through it and tackle his problems tomorrow. But, he had no wool and had not seen any sheep. Red remembered the pig and hoped it was ok in the dark.

A hissing sound made him freeze. Glowing red eyes appeared out of the darkness and headed straight for him! He raised his sword and with one hard blow defeated the spider. More hissing came from the side and another spider jumped at him. Red ducked to avoid being hit and plunged his sword into the creature. He collected the string it dropped and sprinted back to his cave. Even with his new sword, he couldn't fight all night. Without shelter, he was a goner.

The torches he put in the cave helped him find his way, but a familiar groaning was coming from the same direction. It wasn't just one zombie – there was a whole group of them!

And they were blocking his way. Red thought about trying to sneak around, but now the hissing was behind him again. He was surrounded! Red needed to run – and fast!

The zombies noticed the lone adventurer and raced toward him. Red sprinted as quickly as his legs could carry, and was able to break through without taking much damage. He dashed into the cave and put up the door just in time. Finally, he could take a breath.

Thud! Crack!

The zombies tore at his wooden door, trying to get to him. Red had no idea if it was strong enough to hold them off, but he had no choice.

Bang! Smash!

The door shuddered with each blow. It was going to break!

Red had to think quickly. He couldn't go anywhere but...an idea struck him. First, he constructed a booth with four walls. Then, he took out his pickaxe and began to mine down. Red did not know if the invisible wall also stretched underneath, but he had to try.

Since his cave was so small, he had to go block by block. The first rule of Minecraft is to never mine straight down. You might fall into a dungeon – or even worse, lava. With each block he descended lower and lower, placing torches to light the way.

"AAAH!" Red couldn't help but yell. He almost stepped off a perfectly safe dirt block into nothingness. Next to him was a long way down. He could see the red and yellow pools of lava on the bottom. This was where he had to stop.

Red covered the gaping hole with dirt and waited.

Crash!

His door was destroyed! The zombies piled into his cavern. Red stayed very quiet, hoping they would just leave. Unable to find their prey, the zombies got very angry. They stayed around for a while, but soon Red couldn't hear them at all. They must have finally left, he assumed. Light began to show at the top of the booth and he realized it was daytime again. Relieved he survived the horrible night, Red began to make his way back up.

The day was just beginning. Red peeked out and saw zombies on fire running around outside his cave. If he wasn't in such a dire situation, he would have laughed. But this was no time for laughing. He was trapped in this place, and unless he found some sand, he would never see his home again.

When the coast was clear, Red went over to the unfinished building near the gate. The first order of business was to make a shelter to withstand another zombie attack. He mined many cobblestone blocks and put up solid walls. He couldn't make windows because he had no glass, so he ended up leaving a square hole in the ceiling to make sure he knew when the sun was coming up. Red dug a small tunnel right underneath in case in rained and also dug a mote around the house filled with water. That way, no mobs could surround him. Before nightfall, he would destroy the bridge and sleep soundly.

Speaking of sleeping, Red remembered he collected some string from the spiders he killed. Now he could make a bed! Red crafted the bed and placed it in his new home. The house didn't look too shabby, and he was proud of his work. He moved the crafting table and furnace inside, and put torches everywhere he could. Darkness wouldn't scare him again!

When his work was complete, Red began to mine. He wanted to find a safe way into the underground cave he found earlier. Maybe there would be something he could use. After hours of hard work, Red sat down to have a snack and replenish his food bar. His pickaxe was also wearing out. Red was enjoying the sunny weather and his apple when suddenly a scream filled the air.

"HELP!"

# CHAPTER 3: A FRIEND IN NEED

Red jumped up and sprinted towards the sound. A million thoughts raced through his head. Who was yelling? Why did they need help? Does this mean he wasn't alone here?

"AAAH! HELP!" the same voice cried out. Red was almost to it. When he spotted the source, he couldn't believe his eyes. One...two...no, *three* skeletons were shooting arrows at a cowering blue figure in the grass.

And the worst part was they were wearing helmets! Where in the world did they get helmets? But Red had no time to speculate. Even though the person being shot at was wearing diamond armor it wouldn't last forever against three attackers. The arrows were bouncing off for the moment, so Red came up with a plan.

He carefully sneaked around the trees and hid behind the first mob. The skeleton was busy flinging arrows at its victim so it didn't notice. Red lunged forward and hit its bony body with a mighty blow from his sword. Shocked, the skeleton turned around and tried to defend itself. Red swung again and again. Even with a helmet, the skeleton had no chance. It was quickly defeated.

The sound of fighting attracted the attention of the others. They turned to Red and began firing arrows at him.

"Run!" he yelled out, but the armored person didn't move. Red dodged the arrows as he approached the second skeleton. Once between them, he ducked as an arrow narrowly missed his head – and stuck right in the other skeleton's body. Red kept running, but his plan worked. The injured skeleton began shooting back at the one who hit it until they both destroyed each other. Red collected the bones and arrows that dropped and then went over to check on his new companion.

"Are you ok?" Red asked. "The skeletons are gone now. You're safe."

The person finally stood up, and Red saw that it was an adventurer boy just like him.

"Really?" he asked. "Wow. Thanks a lot!"

"No problem," Red replied. "I'm Red."

"I'm G...Gil. My name's Gil," the boy stumbled.

"Nice to meet you, Gil," Red said. "Do you remember how you got here?"

Gil shook his head no.

"The last thing I remember is I was uh...making some helmets and uh...the next moment I'm getting attacked by three skeletons!"

"I saw that," Red confirmed, "but why didn't you just fight them? It looks like you still have your armor and there's a diamond sword on your hip. You could have taken them no problem!"

Gil looked away in shame.

"I was scared," he admitted. "I'm not a fighter. This stuff was all uh...a gift. I've never actually used it before."

That seemed very strange to Red. Diamonds were expensive so it was unlikely someone would just give them away. Maybe he's a griefer and stole the armor, Red thought, but Gil seemed too cowardly to rob anyone. No, he had to be telling the truth.

"It's ok," Red reassured him. "Maybe I can teach you how to fight."

"That would be awesome!" exclaimed Gil.

"But first," said Red, "we need to find a way out of here."

"What do you mean?" asked Gil.

"This isn't an ordinary place," Red explained. "We were somehow transported to the Tutorial. I tried to complete it so the invisible wall around us disappears, but now I'm stuck. The next step is to craft glass, but there's no sand, only sandstone, around the water. Since it looks like you retained your inventory, you don't happen to have any sand on you?"

"No, sorry," Gil said, frowning. "So what do we do?"

Red looked at Gil's diamond getup and an idea popped into his head.

"There's lava in a cave under us. If we can get down there, you can mine obsidian and create a portal to the Nether. From there, we can travel to a desert and mine some sand to bring back."

"The Nether?" Gil yelled, his eyes going wide. "That place is way too dangerous!"

"It's our only option," Red said. "Do you have another idea?"

Gil didn't.

"If we can escape to other biomes through the Nether, why not just stay there?" he asked.

"Because if something happens to one of us, we'll be spawned back here with no inventory," Red answered. "Plus, if you and I were trapped, what if someone else is teleported here too? I can't let that happen. We have to complete the Tutorial."

Gil reluctantly agreed and Red took him to his mining shaft. Torches lined the walls as they descended deeper and deeper underground. Red and Gil used their pickaxes until an opening appeared into a large cave. They could finally see the lava pools below. It was still a pretty steep drop so they descended a ladder first.

"I don't wanna go!" Gil whined as he felt the heat coming off the lava.

"Don't worry," Red told him, "I will protect you. But we need this obsidian and I need your diamond tools to mine it."

"Ok," Gil conceded. They jumped on the stone floor of the cave and looked around. It seemed empty, until…

# CHAPTER 4: TRAINING FOR OBSIDIAN

"Watch out!" Gil screamed as a cave spider emerged from behind a wall. It leaped on Red, who didn't have time to react. He was bit! Gil was about to run but Red was injured. Without him, Gil was definitely going to die. Gil closed his eyes and began swinging wildly with his diamond sword. The cave spider was struck and destroyed. Amazed at his victory, Gil quickly gave Red some milk to combat the spider's poison. Soon, Red was back to normal.

"Thanks!" he told Gil. "You were very brave."

"You really think so?" Gil said.

"Yes. You didn't run. You stayed and helped your friend. That's bravery," Red explained.

"We're...friends?" Gil asked with surprise.

"Sure, why wouldn't we be?" asked Red. Gil shuffled his feet shyly.

"I've just never had a real friend before," he confessed.

"Well you do now," smiled Red. Gil smiled back happily.

"It's a good thing you had milk for this poison," Red said. "I used to always keep some in my inventory too, just in case. I'm ok now. We can keep going."

Gil only nodded in response, his smile fading.

They continued through the cave, looking for a place that had both water and lava so they could make obsidian.

"I see something blue over there!" cried Gil. He was right! They found an underground waterfall right next to a lava pool. It was the perfect place.

PLOP. PLOP. PLOP.

"Uh oh," said Red. "I know that sound. It's a slime."

"Where?" Gil yelped. His eyes darted around in fear.

PLOP. PLOP.

The slime seemed to be getting closer. It must have heard them. Gil and Red came to a narrow stone archway and behind it was a giant green creature throwing itself at the blocks.

"It's too big," Red gathered. "It won't be able to get through."

"Are you sure?" Gil asked, his voice shaking as he watched the slimy mob from a distance.

"Yes," Red assured him, "but, I think this is the perfect time for you to get some practice with your sword."

"Huh?" Gil's eyes went wide and he almost dropped his weapon.

"It can't hurt you but we need to get to the other side of that archway. I promised I would teach you how to fight, so here is my first lesson." Red took out his own stone sword and held it in front of him in an attacking position.

"Hold it like this. Always keep your eyes on the mob. Then, strike as hard as you can!" He swung the sword through the air. It made a whooshing sound and Gil backed away instinctively. "Your turn!"

Gil tried to follow Red's instructions. He lifted the diamond sword and did some practice swings. At first they were weak, but Gil kept going until his blows were filled with power.

"Good job!" Red praised. "You're a fast learner!"

Gil glowed with pride. "Thanks!"

"Now it's time to take care of that slime," said Red.

Gil suddenly lost his confidence.

"I don't know," he said. "I don't think I'm ready."

"If you don't try, you'll never find out."

"Alright," Gil conceded. He walked over to the archway and got in position. His whole body shook as he looked into the black eyes of the giant green monster.

PLOP. PLOP. PLOP.

"Remember, you can't close your eyes," Red coached. "You have to aim. If you accidentally hit the archway, the slime will get through."

Gil set his sights on the slime and with a deep breath swung his sword. The powerful blow hit the slime and threw it back.

"Nice!" Red yelled. "Keep swinging! It's damaged but not destroyed. Most mobs don't go down with one hit, even with a diamond sword."

Gil swung again, and this time the slime was defeated.

Or so he thought!

"What's going on?" Gil cried out as little slime chunks made their way through the archway – and right towards him!

"When a slime is destroyed, it spawns little drops," Red explained quickly. "You have to finish them off!"

"AAAH!" Gil screamed as he hit each one with his sword until they were all gone. He plopped down on the ground, exhausted.

"Great job," Red told him, impressed. "You'll make a great warrior someday."

Gil was tired but he was also thrilled to have defeated such a great foe all on his own. He ate an apple to replenish his strength.

"Let's keep going," he said. "I don't want to stay here longer than we have to."

Red nodded and they walked through the archway.

The lava pool and waterfall were just close enough for Red to place a few blocks of dirt in between. Then he cut off the water and they turned to obsidian! Gil mined it with his diamond pickaxe until they had enough to make a few nether portals. Red crafted one and Gil lit it with some flint and steel from his inventory. The ominous purple swirls of the vortex scared Gil, but Red seemed to know what he was doing.

Red jumped in and disappeared. Not wanting to be alone, Gil closed his eyes and followed. How bad could it be?

# CHAPTER 5: NEW NETHER FRIENDS

Red and Gil emerged in the fiery redness of the Nether. There was lava everywhere! Lava pools, lava ponds, and even lavafalls! The sky was completely black and fields of netherrack covered the ground.

"This is a very dangerous place," warned Red. "We have to stick together."

"It's so hot here!" Gil complained. He wiped sweat off his forehead.

"I know," Red agreed. "Let's leave a beacon so we know where the portal back is and start walking."

He built a tall tower and put a torch on top. That way they could see it from almost anywhere. Unfortunately, the mobs could see them too!

"Watch out!" screamed Gil. Red was all the way at the top when a white jellyfish creature floated up to him. It opened its gaping mouth and spit out a ball of red hot flames. Red expertly drew his sword and hit the fireball straight back into the ghast. It let out a high pitched squeal before BOOM! The creature exploded into white puffs of smoke!

"Wooooaaah!" Red let out as he struggled to keep balance. Falling would mean certain death. The last thing he wanted to do was respawn back in the Tutorial with no inventory again. Luckily, he didn't fall. Carefully, he climbed back down and met up with Gil.

"I thought you were a goner!" Gil cried.

"It'll take a lot more than one ghast to take me down," boasted Red.

"Be careful what you wish for!" said Gil as he raised his sword. Red turned around to see what Gil was talking about.

OINK. OINK.

A zombie pigman was standing on a nearby platform! It was armed with a golden sword.

"No! Stop!" Red yelled to Gil, but it was too late. Gil struck the pigman with his diamond sword, enraging the mob. The pigman let out a loud shriek and began to advance on Gil. It blocked Gil's next blow and landed its own. If that wasn't enough, three more zombie pigmen came out of nowhere and surrounded Red and Gil!

"Where did *they* come from?" Gil cried as he defended with all his might.

"Zombie pigmen are neutral mobs that spawn in fours," Red explained, swinging his sword at the attackers. "They don't agro unless you hit them first, but once you do everyone goes after you."

Oh no, Gil thought, this was all his fault! He had to make it right. Gil focused on the techniques he learned from Red and with a massive blow from his sword finally took down one of the pigmen. Red saw his determination and fought ever harder. Working together, they destroyed all four mobs.

"I'm sorry I almost got us killed," Gil apologized. "I guess you don't want to be my friend anymore."

"That's silly," Red said. "Everyone makes mistakes. That's how we learn not to make them again."

"No matter how bad?" Gil asked, his eyes hopeful.

"Yup," answered Red. "Uh-oh. We do have a small problem."

"What's wrong?"

"My sword," Red said, showing Gil his weapon. "It's almost broken. One more fight and it'll be useless."

"We have to craft you another one!" cried Gil. He didn't like the idea that Red was unarmed. Actually, now that he thought about it, he didn't like that Red had no armor either. Red had been helping him all this time and Gil didn't even think about his friend's health.

"Here," Gil said, "I have some golden ingots in my inventory. Take them and craft a sword and armor for yourself. It's not very fair that I'm walking around with diamond protection while you're completely vulnerable."

He handed Red a stack of golden ingots. Red looked at them thoughtfully.

"Are you sure?" he asked Gil. "These were probably really hard to get. I know, I mined for gold all the time."

"I'm sure," Gil answered, looking down on the ground. "You're my friend and friends take care of each other."

Red thanked Gil and took the ingots. Luckily, he brought his crafting table along and forged himself a brand new golden sword and full set of golden armor. It wasn't as good as his lost diamond items, but he was still glad to have it.

"HELP!" A cry echoed in the distance.

Red and Gil jumped up and looked around.

"Somebody! Anybody! Help!"

Without a second thought, they sprinted towards the sound. Soon, they came upon a huge river of lava and in the middle was an island of just four blocks – with three people standing on it!

"Help us!" called out the girl in the group. "We're struck!"

Lava boiled all around them. Gil turned to Red with a questioning look.

"What do we do?" he asked.

"We have to make a bridge," Red responded. He began to mine nearby netherrack and dropped the collected blocks into the lava. Gil followed suit and made a second row for a wider path. The pathway got closer and closer to the trapped trio.

"Hurry!" the girl yelled. "There's a magma cube swimming towards us!"

Red looked over at the lava and saw that she was right. A large black and red cube was quickly making its way to the island. He mined as fast as he could and just as the magma cube bounced on top of its prey the last block was laid and the three escaped down the makeshift pathway.

But they weren't out of the woods yet! The magma cube sprung up into the air like a slinky and followed them. Red and Gil drew their swords and got ready. The cube jumped and aimed for Gil. Gil swung and hit it away with a mighty blow. It quickly recovered and bounced again, but Red struck it and the magma cube split apart. Except now there were a bunch of smaller cubes coming at them!

"This is just like the slime!" Gil exclaimed.

They hacked at the mobs, and the small ones turned to tiny cubes with glowing eyes. It was ridiculous! When every spawn was destroyed, Gil and Red were exhausted. They sat down and ate some food.

"Thank you so much!" the rescued girl told them. "I'm Roxy. And this is Hunter and Chase." She pointed to the guys standing beside her.

Red nodded at them in greeting. "I'm Red and this is Gil. What happened to you guys?"

"And why are you in the Nether with no armor or weapons?" wondered Gil.

"We were griefed," spoke up Hunter. His voice was low and full of anger.

"Yeah," added Chase. "They took everything! We've spent hours here mining and collecting useful resources to take home. Then these two guys in enchanted diamond armor show up and tell us if we don't hand over our stuff they would destroy us."

"We tried fighting," Roxy continued, "but it was no use. Our blows did nothing to them. In the end we chose to give up the items, and then they took our friend Allie and trapped us in the middle of the lava!"

"That's terrible!" cried Gil. He couldn't believe someone could be so cruel.

"We have to find her," Roxy said. "She must be so scared being a prisoner of those griefers."

"Where did they take her?" asked Red.

"To the Nether Fortress," Chase answered. "They're probably planning to use her as a trap tester. There are many chests with all kinds of loot in there, but some are booby trapped. Poor Allie."

"We should have never let them take her!" roared Hunter.

"Well what did you expect us to do, smart guy?" retorted Roxy.

"Everybody calm down," Red intervened. "We'll help you get your friend back."

"You will?" asked Roxy.

"We will?" asked Gil.

"Yes," said Red. "We'll go into the Nether Fortress and rescue her from these griefers. Maybe the four of you couldn't take them on, but Gil has diamond armor and I'm an expert swordsman. If we work together, we can defeat any foe."

"He's right," chimed in Chase. "Arguing won't help Allie."

"But how are we supposed to defend ourselves?" asked Hunter. It was a good question.

"Our portal is nearby," said Red. "We can go in and mine for some materials to make everyone armor and weapons."

"We don't have time for that!" Hunter bellowed. "Allie could be walking into a trap as we speak!"

"Well," Red considered, "I did have a few golden ingots left after crafting my items, but there's only enough to make swords. *And* they belong to Gil, so you'd have to ask him."

Everyone turned and looked at Gil.

"Please," begged Roxy. "We'll do anything! We'll be your best friends forever!"

Hunter rolled his eyes.

"We'll owe you one," he said. "Well, *another* one."

"And we'll pay back triple," added Chase.

Gil didn't like being put on the spot like that, but he really did want to help them. Plus, he liked the idea of having more friends.

"Sure," Gil decided and handed over the golden ingots. The three cheered and Roxy hugged him. Red crafted three golden swords and handed them out.

"Alright, now we're ready," he said, and the group set out on their rescue mission towards the Nether Fortress.

# CHAPTER 6: LENDING A HELPING HAND

"So, what are you guys doing here?" Chase asked Red and Gil as they walked cautiously to the dark looming structure.

"We were somehow spawned in the Tutorial biome," answered Red. "But it's not normal. Little things are different, like a bunch of apples falling out of trees at once and all sand turned to sandstone. I tried to complete it so the invisible wall disappeared but the next step required me to make glass. Without sand it was impossible so we created the nether portal in order to find a sand biome and bring some back."

"Wow," pondered Chase. "That's weird."

"It sounds like the work of the Glitcher," said Hunter.

"The Glitcher?" asked Red.

"Yeah, he's the worst griefer of all," Hunter explained. "The Glitcher changes the root code of each biome to wreak havoc and destruction. I heard that sometimes he creates bugs so bad they crash the entire world!"

"Why would somebody do that?" asked Roxy.

"I don't know," shrugged Hunter. "Maybe he enjoys seeing people angry and upset. Why would those other griefers rob us and take our friend?"

"It sounds a little out there," argued Red. "If the Glitcher wanted to hurt me, he could have done a lot worse than some apples and a puzzle. What do you think, Gil?"

"I uh…think that maybe you shouldn't believe everything you hear," Gil reasoned.

"Maybe he's just playing harmless pranks. Maybe he's just...lonely."

Hunter rolled his eyes. "Yeah right. Griefers are all scum. I wish they would all just go away and leave us *regular* people alone. No one likes to get griefed, no matter if it's a prank or not."

"That's true," admitted Red. "But I also agree with Gil. We shouldn't jump to conclusions."

"You do what you want," said Hunter and sprinted ahead.

"We actually live in the desert," Roxy said. "If you want, after we rescue Allie, we can take you home and you can have all the sand you want."

"Thanks," replied Red. "We'll take you up on that offer, right Gil?"

"Sure," said Gil, but his voice seemed sad.

"What's wrong?" asked Red.

"It's nothing," Gil answered. "I'm uh... just thinking about how dangerous the Nether Fortress is."

Red didn't believe him. He could tell there was something else on Gil's mind, but he didn't want to push. They were almost at the fortress when Hunter suddenly stopped. "Look out!"

Two ghasts came out of nowhere and started shooting fireballs at the group. One went straight for Roxy! She deflected it with her sword and the ghast exploded with a wail, dropping a ghast tear she quickly picked up. The second jellyfish creature was still spitting out attacks and setting fire to blocks all around. It stayed floating just far enough out of reach. Since no one had bows and arrows it was impossible to destroy unless they could redirect another fireball. Just when Red was ready to jump and hit one, five more ghasts showed up! They were outnumbered!

"We need to get inside!" Red instructed. "The ghasts can't follow us there!"

Without arguing, everyone sprinted for the Nether Fortress. They ran up the giant set of stairs made from nether brick. As soon as they passed the doorway, the ghasts stopped chasing them.

"How did you know they would do that?" asked Gil, trying to catch his breath.

"Ghasts can't survive in enclosed spaces," Red answered. He was very familiar with creatures in the Nether since he had traveled there many times.

"Well, I'm glad we're safe now," said Chase.

"I wouldn't be so sure!" shouted Hunter.

A bright yellow blaze hovered above them, its black eyes staring straight at Red. The monster waited a moment and then unleashed three fireballs. There was no way to deflect all of them, so Red rolled away from the attack. One of the blows nicked his shoulder and his health bar dipped.

"Oh no, Red's hurt!" Gil cried. He raised his diamond sword and lunged at the blaze. He hit it over and over, but it wasn't enough. The blaze's health was just too high! Seeing Gil struggle, Chase and Hunter came to his side. They attacked the blaze while dodging its fiery blows until it was finally destroyed.

"Are you ok, Red?" asked Gil as he ran to his friend's side. He handed Red a potion of healing and stayed with him until the whole thing was gone.

"I'm good," said Red. "Thanks. We can keep going now."

But Gil wasn't sure it was such a good idea anymore. If one blaze did so much damage, what else lurked in these dark shadows? He shuddered at the thought.

"Maybe-" he began, but a loud scream echoing from somewhere deep inside the fortress interrupted him.

"What was that?" asked Red.

"It was Allie!" cried Roxy. "I'd recognize her voice anywhere!"

"Let's hurry!" said Hunter as he ran towards the sound.

"Hey, wait for us!" yelled Chase, and the rest of the gang followed Hunter into the darkness.

## CHAPTER 7: TREASURE TRAPS

"AAAAH!" The scream got louder and louder. The group climbed a huge staircase lined with red flowers of Nether Wart. Even though there were no torches, a light emanated from the unique blocks so they could see their way. They came to a huge cave with lavafall pillars all around. At the center stood three pedestals with treasure chests. The rescuers slowly came forward and saw a hole in front of the middle chest – and inside it was a girl surrounded by lava!

"Allie!" cried Roxy.

"Roxy!" Allie shouted back. "You guys came to save me!"

"We sure did!" said Hunter. "What happened?"

"The griefers made me open the treasure chests, one by one. The first was no problem but the middle one was booby trapped! I fell in and now I'm stuck with nowhere to turn!"

"We'll get you out of there," Hunter promised and began to dig down to her.

"Where are the griefers?" asked Chase, looking around nervously.

"I think they ran as soon as I fell," Allie guessed. "They were probably afraid it was wired to explode."

"Well good thing it wasn't."

"You got that right!"

A few minutes later Allie was safely out of the hole. She hugged her friends and told them thank you. Then she saw the two strangers.

"Who are you guys?" she asked.

"This is Red and Gil," said Roxy before they could answer. "They saved us from being destroyed by a magma cube! *And* they crafted us these golden swords so we could come recue you!"

"Wow," Allie said, impressed. "Thanks, guys!"

Red smiled. "No problem."

"So what now?" asked Gil.

"I want to go aftcr the griefers!" roared Hunter. "They need to pay for what they did! And give us back our stuff."

"No way," Allie protested. "I'm not going after anyone! I want to go home!"

"I'm with Allie," Roxy agreed. "This place is trouble. We should go home and craft armor and weapons so next time we won't be caught off guard."

"You guys are all chickens," Hunter taunted. "Don't you want revenge?"

"I understand why you're angry," said Red, "but putting your friends in danger will only make things worse. What if someone gets hurt? Is it really worth the risk?"

He could see that Hunter was a good person and was only trying to make up for failing to protect his friends earlier.

"I guess," Hunter said with a sigh. "Let's go home."

"Alright!" cheered Allie and Roxy. Even Chase smiled.

"What about this last chest?" asked Gil, eyeing the third treasure. He had never seen one before and really wanted to know what was inside.

"I wouldn't open it," said Allie. "Not after what happened with this one."

"To be fair," Red reasoned, "there's a low chance of it being a trap since we already triggered the main one. If the first chest was clear, I would guess the third one is too."

"I'll do it," offered Gil. "My armor is the strongest so if it is a trap, I have the best chance of survival."

"You don't have to," Red told him.

"I know," said Gil, "I want to! I don't know if I'll ever get another chance at an adventure like this."

"Ok. Everyone get back," warned Red. The foursome moved away from the treasure chest. Gil walked up to the lid and checked for any tripwires or pressure plates. He didn't see any so he took a deep breath and opened the chest.

A creak was heard in the distance and a small opening appeared on the side of the room. Gil didn't notice because he was busy staring at the mountain of treasure! There were gold ingots, obsidian – and even diamonds! He couldn't believe his eyes!

"This is awesome!" Gil exclaimed. "Check out all this loot!"

"Um, Gil?" said Red in a low voice. "You might want to turn around."

Confused, Gil followed Red's stare and froze. Charred skeletons with stone swords were pouring out of the hole in the wall!

"It's an ambush!" cried Chase.

"We got this," Hunter said, raising his sword.

Allie hid behind Roxy since she didn't have a weapon. The others armed themselves and got ready for the impending attack. The wither skeletons sprinted towards them and struck.

Hunter and Chase fought hard, plunging their swords into the skeleton bodies. Red and Gil also landed powerful blows on the mobs, destroying one after the other. Roxy defended her friend with all her might, but three wither skeletons surrounded her and one landed an attack. It applied the Wither effect, a horrible debuff that drains health. Red stepped up to help her and fought the skeletons while Gil gave her some milk to drink.

"I don't know how much longer we can hold out!" shouted Hunter through the battle.

"We have to close the trap!" realized Gil.

"But how?" asked Chase.

"We can stand back to back and move to the trap door," proposed Red.

"Yes!" added Gil. "And when we're there, I can block it with obsidian!"

They banded together and began to execute the plan. They moved quickly through the skeletons, leaving no weak spots, until they finally reached the door. Gil dropped the obsidian and blocked any more mobs from coming in. They fought the rest of the wither skeletons until the last one was destroyed. It was a challenging battle, and everyone was tired and hungry at the end. They took a moment to rest, and Red gave out the rest of his apples.

"Thanks again," said Roxy. "I'm starting to lose count of how many favors we owe you."

Red considered her words. "Thank the Glitcher. If it wasn't for him, I wouldn't have all these apples."

"And we wouldn't have been here to save you guys," commented Gil.

"I guess everything has a silver lining," conceded Hunter. "But it still doesn't make what he did ok."

"That's true," agreed Red.

When everyone was fed and rested, the group cautiously walked out of the Nether Fortress. Red and Gil followed their new friends to their home. Upon reaching the portal, Roxy looked it over with suspicion.

"There's something different about it," she said. "Besides the fact that it's been deactivated."

"I don't see anything strange," said Hunter. "It was probably damaged by a ghast. We can just relight it."

Roxy sighed. "I guess."

"Let's go!" urged Allie. Gil used his flint and steel to reactivate the portal and soon he was staring at the familiar purple swirls.

"Geronimooo!" yelled Hunter and jumped in the portal. The rest of the gang followed, ending with Red and Gil. They were finally out of the Nether...

# CHAPTER 8: HOME IS WHERE THE OCELOT IS

. . . and standing completely soaked in a thunderstorm!

"Rain? I thought it didn't rain in the desert!" said Gil as he tried to see through the wall of water surrounding him. All he could make out was greenery everywhere.

"That's because this *isn't* the desert!" cried Roxy. "I *knew* there was something fishy about that portal!"

"It must have been those griefers!" Hunter shouted angrily. "I'm going to get them for this!"

"We need to find shelter," Red said, studying his surroundings. They looked very familiar.

"I see something up ahead! Looks like the side of a cliff. We could dig a cavern," suggested Chase.

The wet group trudged to the dirt wall and began to dig. Soon, they were out of the rain and in a shallow cave. Red put up some torches for warmth and they waited for the storm to pass.

Roxy looked excited. "I wonder where we are!"

"I think we're in the jungle biome," said Red.

"How do you know?" asked Allie.

"Because that's where I'm from. I recognize this area. My house is pretty close to this cliff side."

"Oh wow! The jungle!" exclaimed Roxy. "Isn't that where ocelots live?"

"That's right. They're everywhere around here."

"I've always wanted a kitty!" she squealed.

"Me too!" Allie joined her.

"Do you have one?" Roxy asked Red.

"No," he said. "I've thought about it since they scare off creepers, but I'm always away on adventures and exploring so I decided a pet wasn't a good idea. I wouldn't want it to get lonely."

"I guess I understand that," agreed Roxy, "but mine would never be alone since my house is in a village. I really want to tame one!"

"I'll help you," offered Red.

"Can you help me too?" asked Allie.

"Sure," said Red. He turned to Chase and Hunter. "How about you guys?"

"No thanks," replied Hunter. "I'd rather tame a wolf."

"Me too," added Chase.

"I'd like one," Gil said quietly.

"Of course," Red told him. "You know Gil, you never told me where you're from."

Gil shifted uncomfortably.

"I live in a village of a forest biome," he began. "We have lots of trees and tall grass. My house is pretty small but the villagers provide everything I need so I don't have to travel anywhere, and an iron golem protects us from mobs so it's safe."

"That sounds nice," Allie said.

Hunter scoffed. "It sounds *boring*."

"You guys live in a desert!" Gil defended. "What's so fun about endless sand and prickly cactuses?"

"I'll tell you!" Hunter countered. "We have desert temples! They are *full* of treasure. But you'd have to be an expert not to fall for their traps."

Gil was about to say something else but Red stepped in.

"Stop it, you guys. Let's leave the fighting for the hostile mobs, ok?"

"Sorry," said Gil, his face turning red in embarrassment.

Hunter rolled his eyes. "Fine."

"Look!" cried Roxy. "The rain is gone!"

The group looked out and realized that the weather had finally cleared up. They were free to leave the cave. Red led them through the tropical biome of vines and leaves, up and down the lush hilly landscape, around large tall jungle trees, and through lakes nestled in valleys.

"It's so beautiful here!" exclaimed Allie. "I would love to live in a place like this!"

"Sure," huffed Hunter, "if it wasn't so uneven. If I have to walk up another hill I'm going to explode like a creeper!"

"We can take a break and eat as soon as we get to my house," said Red. "It's just around this next ravine."

Red was right – as soon as they passed a narrow gorge, a large structure of cobblestone and moss appeared. It was smack dab in the middle of a pond with only a two block wide bridge leading inside.

"Woah!" cried Chase. "That's a jungle temple!"

Red only smiled and led them closer. He stopped right before the doorway and disabled the tripwire.

"I didn't want any unwelcomed guests so I booby trapped the door," he explained. A stone entrance opened and allowed them in.

Red's house was fully furnished, not at all like it looked on the outside. It actually felt very homey, thought Gil. Red offered to get food from a chest in his cellar, so he told everyone to stay put while he went to get it.

Of course Hunter was too curious and decided he wanted to explore instead. After Red was out of sight, he went downstairs and saw three levers. He didn't know what they did so he decided not to push them. Hunter kept going until he saw a different corridor, but as soon as he turned he heard a *click*. Uh-oh, he thought, but it was too late! An arrow whizzed right past his face! Hunter ducked with a yelp and scrambled across the floor until he was out of line of sight of the dispenser. Whew! He was glad no one saw him. Hunter didn't want to encounter any more traps so he went back up to join the rest of his friends, who were safely eating some melons.

"Did you find what you were looking for?" asked Red with a grin.

"Haha, very funny," said Hunter, before biting into a juicy melon.

Soon everyone was full and rested. Red offered to let them stay the night and continue the quest tomorrow, but Roxy and Allie wanted to go look for ocelots. Sunset was still a little ways off so he agreed to help.

First, they had to collect some fish to tame the ocelots with. Red gave Gil, Roxy, and Allie fishing rods and they each caught several fish.

Allie grimaced. "Ew! They're so slimy! I hope I don't have to hold on to them for long."

"Yeah," agreed Roxy. "And they're stinky. Pee-yew!"

"Don't worry," Red reassured them. "The ocelots will gobble them all up."

The foursome went in search for the jungle cats. They listened for distant meows and colorful patches in the leaves. After a little while, the first ocelot showed its little orange face.

"It's so cute!" squealed Allie.

"Shh!" shushed Red. "You have to be quiet and stay back so you don't startle it. Just take out the fish and let it come to you."

"Oh, ok." She held the raw fish out to the ocelot and waited. At first, the kitty just sniffed around, and seeing no danger it came closer and closer to Allie. She vibrated with excitement but stood very still. The ocelot grabbed the fish and ran!

"No! Come back!" she yelled after it with dismay. Tears began to form in her eyes.

Red tried to comfort her. "It's ok, Allie. Sometimes it takes more than one try. You can do it. Believe in yourself."

Allied nodded and took out another fish. She inched closer and closer to the elusive ocelot until it noticed her.

"Here kitty kitty," she sang. The ocelot walked up to her again and began to eat the fish, but this time it stayed instead of running. Allie waited with bated breath until – ta-dah! The ocelot turned into a ginger tabby! Allie hugged it and it licked her face, meowing and purring.

"Aw, I love it already!" she exclaimed. "Thank you, Red!"

Red smiled and they went to look for another ocelot. The second one wasn't hard to find, and this time it was Roxy's turn. She followed Red's instructions, and soon tamed a Siamese cat. Lastly, it was Gil's turn, but there were no ocelots to be found! The sky was getting dark and they had to turn around.

"We'll find you one tomorrow, I promise," said Red.

"It's ok," Gil replied with a sigh. They made their way to Red's home. Soon, the familiar structure on the pond was in sights and they sprinted towards it. Darkness was setting in and it was only a matter of time before mobs began to spawn. The temple had torches all around it, but they weren't safe until they were inside those walls.

Running up the bridge, Gil stopped suddenly.

"What's wrong?" asked Red.

"I think I hear something." Gil scanned the dusk. He could have sworn he heard a...

*Meow.*

An ocelot! He spotted it swimming in the pond. Gil took out his fish and held it out to the cat.

"Gil! You need to get inside!" urged Red from his doorway.

Gil's eyes didn't leave the spotted animal. "I can't just leave it here!"

"You have to! It's not safe!"

"Just a little longer," Gil pleaded. The ocelot already noticed the fish and was stalking closer. It began to eat when-

"Watch out!" Red cried. He jumped in front of Gil just as an arrow almost lodged itself in his armor. Red's sword deflected the arrow and he took out his own bow and began to fire at the spawned skeleton on the edge of the bridge.

"Got it!" exclaimed Gil. The ocelot turned into a black cat and meowed at him.

"That's great and all, but you might want to hold off the celebration." Gil looked up and saw a group of mobs making their way up the bridge. He drew his diamond sword and struck the zombie that came at him.

"What's going on out there?" yelled Hunter, peering out from behind the stone door.

"We need some help!" shouted Red. Moments later, Hunter and Chase emerged with swords, while Allie and Roxy stayed back with bows. Red had a stash of weapons in his house and he had no problem sharing with his new friends.

The bridge wasn't wide enough for a real battle, but the mobs didn't care. They heard the noise and kept coming. The group used all their skills to survive, but they were outnumbered. They began to fall back to the house, hoping the stone walls would keep them safe.

"We have to destroy the bridge!" Hunter yelled, but Red was already on top of it. He set a block of TNT, lit it, and ran for his life. The moment the stone door shut, there was a loud BOOM. Red's house shook but stood unharmed. The gang sat quietly and waited to see if any mobs survived on this side but no one came knocking. Relieved, they spent the rest of the night on some of the extra beds Red had. At first, Gil couldn't fall asleep, but his cat (that he named Buddy) curled up around him until Gil finally drifted off.

# CHAPTER 9: THE CREEPY MINE

Morning came and the adventurers were ready to continue on their mission. Gil and Red decided to go look for sand.

"You guys don't have to come," said Red. "If you want, you can go home. We'll be ok."

"Don't you have to go back through the Nether?" asked Roxy.

"And what if those griefers show up?" Hunter chimed in. "You can't take on them yourselves."

"Hunter is right," agreed Chase. "We'll help you get the sand back to the Tutorial. It's the least we can do."

"Not to mention," Hunter continued, "the Tutorial biome is one of the most elusive places in the whole world! It contains endless chests of free loot and treasure. Every explorer dreams of finding their way back after leaving, but it's been proven impossible. Only a glitch made it happen. Don't you see? We can be rich!"

Red considered Hunter's words.

"I don't know if that's such a good idea," he finally said. "The items in the Tutorial are meant for new players, those who need them to start out into the world."

Hunter waved him off. "It's no big deal. They'll just respawn for the next person. No harm no foul."

"I guess," said Red, but he was still uneasy about looting the place.

"What if the Glitcher is still there and does something else to trap us?" asked Allie.

"Don't worry about it," boasted Hunter. "I'll take care of him myself!"

Red shook his head. He just wanted to complete the Tutorial and get back home. If the rest of them decided to stay and collect the chests, that was their choice.

"Do you know where there's some sand?" Gil asked, changing the subject.

Red nodded. "There's a river due west that's surrounded by it." He filled his inventory with all the important things, like food, potions, and tools. He also repaired everyone's weapons and armor before setting out on the expedition. It was important to be prepared.

"You never know what you'll need," Red told them. He also advised that they leave their new pets at his home, as the trip might become dangerous. Roxy and Allie didn't want to, but agreed that it was for the best. They promised the kitties, named Waffles and Sammy, they would be back soon and set out on their journey. But, it wasn't long before Gil heard a *meow* behind him. He looked back to see that Buddy followed him anyway. Red thought about turning back but was assured by Gil that it was no problem, so they continued on.

The sun was high in the sky as they made their way through the thick green grass and leaves of the jungle biome. At one point, Hunter went ahead and Red had to yell for him to stop.

"Be careful!" he warned. "This is very uneven terrain. You can accidentally walk off the top of a cliff or a tree and never know it until you're falling."

Hunter snorted. "I'm smarter than that." But upon taking his next step he suddenly disappeared!

"AAAAAH!" was all the group heard as he fell. They ran up to the place he stood only a moment ago and saw that it was, indeed, the end of a tree top. Many feet below was Hunter, soaking wet and sputtering in the river. Everyone sighed with relief that he was ok.

"Well," shouted a grinning Roxy, "at least you found the river!"

Hunter only grumbled in response.

The gang carefully climbed down on a nearby cliff and came up to the sand that lined the riverbank. Red collected some and put it in his inventory. Now they were ready to go back!

Except...

"Does anyone have obsidian?" asked Red. Everyone shook their heads no.

"I used it all up during our escape from the Nether Fortress," Gil admitted.

"We could try to use the same portal that brought us here," suggested Chase.

"No way," argued Hunter. "If it was made by those griefers, who knows where it would take us next."

"I agree with Hunter," said Red. "I wouldn't risk another griefer trick. We can get some obsidian from a nearby mine."

Red led them through the jungle and to an opening in a cliffside. Several minecarts were sitting on some rails that led inside.

"Ooh!" exclaimed Roxy. "Can we ride it? Please?"

"Sure," said Red. "I built it myself. I discovered this mine a long time ago. The cart will take you all the way down. From there we can get to a cave with lava and water. Then we can make and mine some obsidian."

"Aren't abandoned mines dangerous?" Gil asked nervously.

"Yes," Red replied, "but if we stick together, we can defeat anything we find down there."

Gil nodded, feeling a little better. His friends wouldn't let him down. Allie and Roxy climbed in the cart. Wheee! The cart sped down the rails and out of sight. Next went Hunter and Chase. Lastly, Red, Gil, and Buddy made the trip down.

Gil watched the dark tunnel pass by as the minecart made twists and turns. Torches lined the walls, but it was still dim and pretty scary. He ducked as a cobweb appeared out of nowhere and almost hit him in the face. He was glad when the ride was finally over and they stood at the end of the rails.

"That was so much fun!" shouted Roxy, but Red put his fingers to his lips.

"I wouldn't be too loud," he warned. "There are hostile mobs all over the place. Let's not draw any attention to ourselves."

Roxy nodded and made a zipping gesture across her mouth. They quietly moved down a mineshaft and toward the glistening pool of lava in the distance.

"Eeeew!" squeaked Allie and peeled off a cobweb from her shoulder. "Gross!"

"Where there's cobwebs," said Red, "there's-"

"Cave spiders!" shouted Hunter. Glinting red eyes appeared on the walls, surrounding them. The group drew weapons, ready to defend against the spider attack. Gil and Red slashed at them with swords, destroying one after the other. Hunter and Chase followed suit, striking here and there. Allie and Roxy used their bows to shoot arrows at spiders that were out of reach.

"Ouch!" cried Hunter. "I've been poisoned!"

"There's too many of them," yelled Chase, as he handed Hunter milk. "There has to be a spawner!"

"We need to find it and destroy it, quickly!" instructed Red.

They looked around for a cage with a spider, but didn't see one. The group began to shift down the corridor, until they discovered a side pocket. Inside of it was none other than the cave spider spawner covered in webs! Gil and Red began to clear the cobwebs off the spawner with their swords. When it was finally clear, Gil tried to break the cage, but it seemed invulnerable.

"We have to set it on fire," Red explained. He used a torch and the spawner went up in flames. The spiders finally stopped coming!

"Woohoo!" cheered Roxy. "We did it!"

She gave everyone a high five.

"Let's not get comfortable yet," Red cautioned. "There's still plenty of danger here."

The gang agreed and kept going. They finally reached the large cave that had water and lava. Red made the obsidian while Gil mined it with his diamond sword. The rest of the group looked out for hostile mobs. Roxy shot a skeleton from afar, and Chase took care of a slime. Hunter sat recovering from his poisoned bite, and Allie was standing by to protect him just in case. Buddy swam around in the water, meowing contently. After collecting enough obsidian, they turned back towards the minecart. Luckily, no mobs were in sight until...

"Oh no," whispered Roxy. "What do we do now?"

Right next to the minecart was the most dangerous mob of all - a creeper! Its green body and menacing frown were far enough away not to notice the intruders, but everyone knew what would happen as soon as it did.

"We can't let it see us," Red whispered back. "If it explodes, the track would be ruined and it would take us forever to mine our way out of here. That's *if* we survive."

"Can we destroy it before it blows up?" asked Hunter.

"I don't know," said Red. "And I don't know if I'm willing to take the risk."

"Buddy! Wait!" Gil tried to call out to his kitty friend, but Buddy was already off and heading straight towards the creeper. It jumped in the minecart and meowed. Gil watched with horror as the creeper noticed the feline and...ran! He exhaled with relief, both that the creeper was gone and that his friend was safe.

"Great idea, Gil!" Red praised him. "Creepers are afraid of cats. It's a good thing we kept Buddy or this could have gotten very ugly."

Gil didn't want to tell Red that he forgot about the feline's special power, so he just nodded and joined Buddy in the minecart. Gil leaned close and thanked him. Buddy licked his face and meowed in response. The cart began to move and soon, Gil could see sunshine once again. He had never been so happy. The rest of the group joined him shortly, and they made their way back to Red's home.

## CHAPTER 10: NETHER GRIEFERS

After reuniting Allie and Roxy with their pets, Red crafted a nether portal and activated it. He gave the others a chance to stay, but no one took it. They were friends, and friends helped each other. The group jumped inside the purple swirls and emerged back in the Nether.

It was an unfamiliar place. They looked for high ground so Red could see the beacon he built at their portal. They climbed up a mountain of netherrack, avoiding fire and lava. A ghast emerged from behind but Allie expertly shot it with her arrows before it could even chuck a fireball. The kitties followed their every move, and it made for a cheerier journey through the dark terrain. Once up top, Red saw his beacon and led the way.

They weaved through the lavafalls and narrow passages, slowly closing in on their destination. Hunter almost fell off a bridge when he thought he saw a zombie – which turned out to just be a zombie pigman. This time, Gil knew not to aggravate them. He really did learn from his mistakes, he thought.

The beacon and portal were finally in front of them, but Roxy noticed something was off about *this* one too.

"It's deactivated," she explained. "Like ours was."

Red took a careful look around but didn't see anything out of the ordinary.

"Maybe one of us can go through first," he offered, "and if it's safe, let the others know."

"I wouldn't do that if I were you," a voice appeared behind them. The gang turned around and gasped.

"You!" roared Hunter. Two griefers with enchanted diamond armor stood side by side, shining weapons in their hands.

"Those are the griefers that kidnapped me!" cried Allie.

"And stole our stuff!" added Roxy.

"*And* trapped us in lava!" said Chase.

"What do you want?" Red asked the duo.

"Well," said one of the griefers, "we checked out your portal and found the Tutorial. We also saw that it was bugged and figured out you went to get sand."

"And since you're returning," continued the other, "that means you have the sand to complete it."

"Except you're going to give it to *us*," said the first, "and we're going to finish the instructions and then all the treasure will be ours!"

"No way!" exclaimed Hunter. "We're not afraid of you!"

"Maybe you should be," said the griefer. "Remember what happened last time?"

Hunter drew his sword and charged at the griefers with a battle cry.

"Hunter! Wait!" Red shouted after him, but it was too late. Hunter stepped on a pressure plate and poof! The ground opened up and he was gone. The gang ran forward to see what happened to him and triggered another trap, falling through air and joining their friend. Red looked down and froze.

They were standing smack dab in the middle of an End Portal Frame. Twelve decorated green blocks surrounded them, with eleven eyes of ender inserted in the slots. One more and they would be transported to The End, a place filled with endermen and the ender dragon, the most powerful mob in the entire world.

One of the griefers looked down at them. Red saw an eye of ender gleaming in his hand. "Give us the sand and we won't send you to The End."

"Don't!" Hunter told Red. "He's lying!"

"It's ok," Red assured him. He handed the sand over to the griefers. They took it and smiled.

"Thanks," the griefer said, "but your friend was right. I *was* lying." He threw the last piece in and activated the End Portal. "Have nice trip!"

# CHAPTER 11: THE END OF THE ENDER DRAGON

At first, the group couldn't see anything. The sky was black, and as their eyes adjusted to the low glow of the dimension, they realized that they spawned on a platform of obsidian. Below them was a big island of End stone, and on it walked countless endermen! Pillars of obsidian surrounded the island, but the scariest was a distant roaring sound they knew was none other than the ender dragon.

"Why did you give those griefers the sand?" Hunter complained. "Now they'll take all the loot while we're stuck here!"

Red smiled. "Because it doesn't matter. Only the person who begins the Tutorial is able to complete it. The sand is useless to them."

Hunter perked up. "Hmm, ok. But that still doesn't solve our problem of getting out of here! You know the only way to leave is to defeat the ender dragon!"

"Don't worry," said Red. "I have a plan." He took some pumpkins out of his inventory and handed them out. "Put these on," he directed. "They will make sure the endermen don't attack you."

"Nice!" Roxy said and turned to Allie. "How do I look?"

Allie just laughed and put hers on.

"So, what's the next step?" urged Hunter.

"We have to destroy the ender crystals on the tops of the obsidian pillars. They restore the ender dragon's health. If we want to defeat it we have to get rid of them," Red explained. "Preferably before the dragon notices us."

"Let's split up," Chase suggested. "It would make the job faster."

Red agreed and Allie went with Chase and Hunter, while Roxy stayed with Red and Gil. The girls took aim and pointed their arrows at the ender crystals. They fired and the arrows struck their targets, destroying them. Allie and Roxy cheered and reloaded, shooting again. One by one the crystals exploded, but each time the roar of the ender dragon grew louder and closer. They could see its shadow floating in the darkness. It was only a matter of time before it descended upon them.

Only one crystal remained, but it was too high up to hit. Red began to build a pillar when he heard the dreaded sound of flapping wings behind him.

"Watch out!" cried Roxy. Red turned just in time to see the giant black dragon. The purple eyed beast flew straight at him, its gaping maw ready to strike. Red jumped off the pillar and took some fall damage, but much less than he would have if the ender dragon hit him. The dragon growled in frustration and circled back around. Roxy aimed her bow and hit it, taking a little bit of health and inciting an angry snarl.

"It's too strong!" she told Red. "There's no way we can defeat it!"

"We can," Red assured her, "if we work together."

He drew his sword and stood in a fighting position. When the dragon was near, he jumped out of harm's way and sliced into the creature's body. The dragon howled at being hit and headed to an ender crystal. It began to channel health from it, regaining its strength quickly.

"It's distracted," said Red. "Destroy the last crystal!"

Roxy climbed on top of the pillar and took aim. The arrow flew and hit the crystal head on. Cut off from his healing, the dragon raged and set his sights on her. Roxy carefully jumped down and stood next to Red. The rest of the crew joined them, weapons raised and ready for the fight of their lives.

The dragon swooped down and was met with a barrage of attacks. Swords hit it from all sides, their hard blows taking huge chunks of health. Arrows pierced its scaly skin, sticking inside and causing the dragon to lose strength. The friends fought with all their might, and in the end they were victorious. The ender dragon exploded in beams of purple light, littering the ground with colorful experience orbs. It was defeated!

"Yay! We did it!" cheered Roxy and Allie as everybody took off their pumpkin helmets.

"I can't believe it!" said Hunter.

"Good job everyone," praised Red. "I told you, if we work together, there's nothing we can't do."

"What's this?" Gil asked as he studied a strange bowl-shaped frame of bedrock filled with black liquid. A pillar stood at the center with torches on the sides and an egg on top of it.

"It's the Exit portal," explained Red. "It will take us back to the Overworld."

"And we should go soon," Chase said, looking nervously at the black egg, "before *that* hatches into another dragon."

"Chase is right," Red agreed. "It should take us back to our spawn point."

"But we have no sand!" remembered Gil. "We'll be trapped just like before!"

Red thought about their dilemma.

"You could come with us," offered Roxy.

"Yeah!" said Allie. "There's more of us, so if we all hold hands the portal should take us to *our* home, in the desert biome, instead of the Tutorial."

"That just might work," Red said thoughtfully. "Alright, let's give it a try!"

Hunter grimaced. "Do we have to?" He thought holding hands was for babies.

"It's their only chance," said Roxy. "Plus, how would we get to the Tutorial and all its loot if we lose them now?"

"Alright," grumbled Hunter. "I see your point."

The gang circled the portal and clasped their hands together tightly. Even the kitties held on to their owners. Red began to count.

"One…two…three!"

Everyone jumped inside and let the portal take them – but where?

# CHAPTER 12: A SANDY SURPRISE

"We're HOME!" cheered Roxy. She hugged Waffles and nuzzled his fluffy orange face.

"Finally, a break," said Hunter, relieved they were all there safely.

Red and Gil looked around. They were definitely in the desert, but it wasn't as barren as they expected. They were standing in the middle of a desert village, surrounded by very impressive looking sandstone buildings. And not just that, but small farms of growing food were scattered about. A huge snake-like river circled its way around the biome, providing water for the gardens and citizens. It looked like a great place to live. Gil felt bad for making fun of it to Hunter.

"Wow," said Gil. "This place is awesome!"

"You really think so?" asked Roxy.

"Sure!"

"Come see our house," called Hunter. "It's even better!"

"Just don't step on a cactus," Allie warned. "It hurts!"

Roxy grinned. "One time, Hunter fell into a whole bunch of them and–"

"Hey!" Hunter interrupted her. His face turned red with embarrassment. "It was an accident!" Roxy and Allie giggled but skipped the rest of the story.

They walked along the village, making sure to avoid any cactuses. Villagers passed by and said hello, offering items for sale or trade. Finally, Hunter and Chase stopped in front of a big two-story house with glass windows and a wooden deck.

"Here it is!" Hunter boasted.

Gil marveled at the sight. "So cool!"

"Definitely," Red agreed with him.

"We made it all ourselves," Chase told them. "Come on in!"

They went inside and saw that the interior was just as awesome. There was carpet on the floor, pictures on the walls, a clock, and of course furniture. It felt so homey, Gil never wanted to leave.

"The girls sleep upstairs and our bedrooms are in the back," explained Chase. "There's a guest room if you guys want to spend the night."

"Thank you," said Red, "but I just want to collect some sand and get going. Who knows what kind of havoc those griefers are causing in the Tutorial after realizing they can't complete it."

"No problem, I understand," said Chase. "We'll take you to the river bank so you can mine without disturbing the village."

"Or," Hunter chimed in, "we can go into the desert temple and get some sand *and* treasure."

It was very tempting, but Red knew he needed to focus on his mission. Too much time had already passed since he woke up in the Tutorial, and with each moment something else could go wrong.

"Maybe next time," he promised.

Hunter shrugged. "Suit yourself."

Chase took Red and Gil to the river, and this time they both collected sand. That way, if one lost it, the other would still have some. Buddy swam in the water, enjoying the coolness of it under the hot sun. Unfortunately, they didn't realize just how late it was, and no matter how much Red wanted to leave for the Tutorial, he knew staying the night would be safer. They could get back the next day.

The sun was setting and the villagers returned to their homes. Torches burned all around, preventing mobs from spawning. Red, Gil, and Chase walked briskly to the house. As long as they went inside and fell asleep on the beds, morning would come quick. But luck wasn't on their side. The moment they reached the door, they heard a familiar moaning.

"BUUH!" The growl of a zombie was close - too close! Red drew his sword and spun, swinging it with all his might. The zombie recoiled back but recovered fast and lunged again. Red plunged the sword into the zombie's body and destroyed it.

"BUUUUH!" Another zombie! How many were there? Red saw an iron golem attacking a zombie a few feet away, but there were too many mobs for it to take on by itself. Gil was already swinging his diamond sword, defending against the sea of mobs. Hunter and Chase also came out to help, and Allie and Roxy were standing on the roof of their house with loaded bows, shooting arrows into the monstrous creatures.

HISSSSS

A distant hissing noise put Red on alert. It had to be a creeper! And a creeper meant-

BOOM!

One of the village's buildings exploded!

HISSSSS

BOOM!

Another went up in flames!

"Gil, Roxy, Allie!" shouted Red. "You need to scare those creepers off with your cats before they blow up the entire village!"

Roxy and Allie ran out of the house with Waffles and Sammy on their heels. They split up, sprinting in different directions, hoping that any creepers would notice the felines and run.

"What is going on?" Chase asked Hunter as they plowed down mobs left and right. "We're surrounded by water *and* a fence with torches! There's no way for the mobs to get here!"

"I have no idea," an out-of-breath Hunter replied. "An attack like this has never happened before!"

"We have to find out where they're coming from," advised Red. "Let's go check the perimeter."

"There could be a problem at the bridge," Hunter suggested. "It's the only way in and out."

They agreed to go to it first and the three sprinted across the village, slaying zombies, spiders, and skeletons on the way. They finally reached the bridge that led to the outside of the biome and saw the problem. The torches that lined it were destroyed! Not only that, but the fence gate was gone and remains of another iron golem were scattered about. Someone or something had destroyed it.

Another zombie walked down the bridge and Red defeated it with some powerful blows from his sword. He began to place torches down to keep the mob spawns back.

"Ouch!" cried Hunter. An arrow was stuck in his shoulder! Red looked around and saw glowing red eyes. Except it wasn't just a spider – there was a skeleton riding it! It was a spider jockey, a dangerous combination. Red had to think quickly. He distracted the mob by throwing a rock at it. The aggressive arachnid turned its sights on him, as it had excellent vision in the dark. Chase carried the injured Hunter out of harm's way while Red kept some distance between him and the spider jockey, avoiding its arrows.

"Can you place a new fence gate to block the bridge while I take care of this mob?" Red asked Chase.

"I'm on it!" Chase yelled back and sprinted towards the closest house, hoping there was a crafting table inside.

Red didn't want to get too close to the spider jockey, but he couldn't avoid it forever. He had to destroy it somehow. Suddenly, an arrow buzzed through the air and hit the spider head on! The mob hissed in rage! Another arrow came and the spider was defeated! Red jumped towards the skeleton and stuck it with his sword until it, too, was destroyed. Moments later, he saw Roxy emerge from behind a sandstone house.

"Thanks," he told her.

She smiled back. "No problem!"

Chase soon returned with a freshly crafted fence gate and placed it over the bridge.

"Good, no more mobs should get inside," said Red. "Now we just have to clear the village."

Roxy beamed proudly. "It's already taken care of. Between our arrows, Gil's diamond sword, and the iron golem, they didn't stand a chance!"

"That's great! Then how about we get Hunter home and rest." Red yawned. "I know I need it."

Roxy agreed and they retreated back to their house. Hunter was given a potion of healing and was feeling much better. They finally laid in the comfy beds and soon the whole place shook with snores.

## CHAPTER 13: TUTORIAL COMPLETION

Early in the morning, Red was up and ready to finally finish his quest. His friends were waiting beside him when he activated yet another Nether Portal, with hope that it was his last one for a while. Once the Tutorial was competed, he could find his way home without going through the Nether. His trusty compass would lead the way.

The group emerged once again in the dark red landscape, but this time they were repaired, armed, and fully armored. They knew they had to be ready for the inevitable encounter with the griefers, and possibly even the Glitcher himself. Hunter and Chase carried brand new golden swords, enchanted by the villagers as thanks for defending their home. Even Roxy and Allie's bows were enchanted, one with power and the other with flame. They decided to keep their pets in the village, just in case more creepers came knocking, but promised the kitties they would be back as soon as they helped Red and Gil in their mission.

Together, they had no trouble with the dangerous mobs of the Nether. After fighting off a ghast and magma cube along the way, they reached Red's portal near the beacon. It was still activated from when the griefers went through. They all jumped in and appeared in the simple green landscape of the Tutorial.

"It looks exactly like I remember!" Roxy said.

"Yeah," Allie reminisced. "Even though it's been so long, I can still remember my first spawn like it was yesterday."

"Come on," urged Red. "The instruction sign is this way."

They followed Red to the small clearing near the stone archway. Hunter sucked in a breath.

"Oh man, you guys see all those chests?" he asked with glee, looking beyond the gateway.

"Hold your horses," Roxy told him. "We're not out of the woods yet."

Red carefully took out his sand, and crafted glass while his friends were on the lookout for the griefers. He nervously glanced over at the sign and heaved a sigh of relief. It changed! Now, the instructions were to craft a door. He quickly collected some wood and crafted a door, even though he'd done it before. The steps had to be in order or it wouldn't work. The next guideline was to make torches, which was also very easy. Then, it told him to place the door in a doorway. Red destroyed the door he already had on his small shelter and placed the new one on.

POP! CRACKLE! BANG!

The group jerked up with surprise.

"It's ok," Red tried to calm them. "It's just fireworks!"

The world suddenly lit up with a blinding flash. It quickly dissipated and the sign now read, "Congratulations! You have completed the Tutorial!"

"So we're free now?" asked Gil.

"I think so," Red said.

"Woohoo!" cheered Roxy. "Let's go check it out!"

Hunter sprinted for the archway, and Red thought it would be really funny if the invisible wall was still there. He shook the idea away, remembering his own face meeting it for the first time. It was not funny.

Luckily, they passed through with no problems. Hunter went for the very first chest. It contained a saddle for the dark brown horse that roamed inside the adjoining pen.

"Oooh! I've always wanted to ride a horse!" cried Allie. "I've never done it before."

"I can teach you," said Red. "First, you have to tame it. Ride the horse until it stops trying to throw you off, or you can feed it some carrots."

Allie mounted the horse, but it just neighed loudly and threw her back down. She remembered that taming her ocelot took time and patience, so she tried again. Soon, floating hearts appeared above the animal – it was tamed! Allie equipped it with the saddle so she could steer, and rode the horse around the pen.

"This is so fun!" she squealed. "Do you guys want to try?"

But the rest of the gang were too busy exploring. Roxy opened a chest next to the fountain and it contained a jukebox and a music disc called 'cat'.

"I wonder what it sounds like!" Roxy said and put the disc in the jukebox. A nice upbeat melody filled the air and the friends began to sway their heads to the music. Hunter even broke out some moves, pretending to be a dancing zombie.

"Buuh-buh-buh," he sang along, his arms stretched out wide and moving to the beat. Everyone laughed at his silly rendition. When the song was over, they continued to explore. On the left they collected some food, including carrots and potatoes. Gil took some fish and fed it to Buddy, who happily gulped it down. On the right, they found some enchanting and potion materials. It felt like Christmas morning!

"I want to go to the castle!" said Hunter. "There's bound to be tons of treasure there!"

The others agreed and followed him down the long stone bridge. They crossed the water and reached the huge castle on the other side. Looping around the wall, an entrance appeared. However, inside were several different corridors, leading who-knows-where. They stopped, trying to decide on where to go next.

"I don't think this is a good idea," Gil spoke up, noticing the darkening sky. "We might get lost in here and the night is coming soon. Let's turn around and come back tomorrow."

"Oh come on," groaned Hunter. "Where's your sense of adventure?"

"Gil is right about us needing to be careful," Red said, "but I think I remember there being beds inside. If we stick together and find them quickly, we can wait out the night in here. Then you guys are welcome to do whatever you want tomorrow."

The rest of the group agreed and Hunter was forced to comply. They walked around the maze of the castle, searching every nook and cranny, until finally finding a nice cozy room. Torches lined the walls and it had just enough beds. It was perfect! All it needed was a door, which Red already had in his inventory from the leftovers of the last Tutorial step. He placed it – and not a moment too soon. The sky went dark and noises of rattling, skittering, and grunting were heard from afar. The gang got comfortable in their beds and quickly fell asleep. This was the best day ever!

# CHAPTER 14: THE GLITCHER

"Ummm...guys?" Roxy's worried voice woke the others. Something was different about the room. The stone blocks surrounding them were much darker than before. But something else was making Roxy nervous. She was standing in front of the open door – except there was no hallway behind it. Another wall was blocking their way, made from the same dark blocks. The only exception was a small window in the middle, too small to climb through, but big enough to see that it was daytime outside.

Gil drew his diamond pickaxe and began to mine the stone, but it was no use. He was confused. What could possibly withstand a diamond tool?

"It's bedrock," said Red. "Someone trapped us in here while we were sleeping."

Roxy and Allie gasped in horror.

"Oh no!" whimpered Allie. "How will we get out?"

Hunter seethed. "I bet it was the Glitcher! When I get my hands on him…"

"We don't know that!" Gil objected, but Hunter wasn't listening. He was busy punching at the wall and yelling for the coward to show himself and fight him fairly. Chase tried to calm him down, but it was no use.

"What do we do?" Roxy asked Red.

He shook his head. "I don't know. Wait, I guess."

And so they waited for what felt like forever, but it was really only a few minutes. Then, two familiar faces appeared beyond the window. They smiled wickedly as they saw the group's reaction.

"You guys? *Again?*" Hunter roared.

"You didn't think you'd seen the last of us, did you now?" one of the griefers said.

"Especially not when there's an entire biome full of loot for us to steal," the other added.

"So it was *you* who trapped us here?" Red deduced.

"Who else?" asked the first griefer. "And now, you're going to give us everything you've collected here." An evil grin spread across his face. "If you do, we'll let you out," he promised.

"No way Jose," Hunter protested. "You're crazy if you think we're falling for that again!"

"Suit yourself," the second griefer said. "We'll leave you guys to talk about it and come back later to see if you've changed your mind."

"Yup," his counterpart added, "we got all the time in world. Unlike you."

They laughed and high fived each other before turning back to their prisoners.

"Hey," the left griefer said as his gaze stopped at Gil, "I know you!"

Gil's face went white as he realized his secret was about to be revealed.

The right griefer nodded. "Yeah! I've seen your face on the Griefer Hall of Fame! You're famous, man! What are you doing with *these* losers?"

Red, Hunter, Chase, and the girls all turned to Gil, confused looks on their faces.

"What are they talking about, Gil?" asked Red cautiously.

"I can explain!" Gil tried to defend himself. "It's not what you think!"

"Oh this is priceless," the first griefer teased. "They don't know that you're the G-"

"Stop!" Gil interrupted him. "If you know who I am, you know what I'm capable of! Now you better let me and my friends out or else!"

The griefers exchanged surprised glances, and for a moment Gil thought they would listen.

"Nah," the griefer that almost gave him away said. "If you could have done something, you would have by now. I'm betting you're powerless."

"That's right," his buddy agreed. "Have fun explaining yourself to your so called 'friends'. We'll be back in a few hours for all you guys' stuff."

The griefers waved a mocking goodbye and disappeared behind a corner. Gil was left standing in the middle of the room, trying to figure out what to say.

"Well?" Hunter asked him, waiting for an explanation.

Gil sighed and took a deep breath. "I guess there's no point in hiding it anymore. My name isn't really Gil," he confessed. "It's Glitcher."

He watched everyone's eyes bulge in shock as his friends recoiled from surprise.

"You mean...*the* Glitcher?" Red clarified.

"Yes," Gil confirmed, his eyes shamefully on the floor.

Hunter raised his sword and stood in a defensive position.

"Stay away from us!" he spat. "You're the worst griefer of them all!"

"Now hold on a minute," Red told him, "Gil may be the Glitcher, but he's saved our lives countless times in the last few days. *And* he fought beside us to save your village. Let's hear his side of the story."

Hunter grumbled in response but didn't attack.

"So Gil...err...Glitcher," Red asked, "was it you who trapped me in the Tutorial?"

Gil's eyes were shiny and his voice shook as he answered.

"I was just lonely. I read about you at the Adventurer's Hall of Fame and thought you were really awesome. I wanted to see what you would do when put in an impossible situation. It was just a prank. It's easy to change little things in the root code, like adding sand and stone to make sandstone, or an s to apple to multiply them. I didn't mean any harm and I was going to let you out, really!"

Red nodded in consideration.

"So what happened? How did you end up in there too?"

"I was writing some code so you would find a bunch of armor scattered in the field, but after making the helmets I did something wrong and it threw me inside. The moment I opened my eyes the skeletons were surrounding me. They picked up the helmets and began to attack. I had no idea what to do!"

"You should have let them destroy him!" Hunter told Red through gritted teeth.

"And your inventory? The diamond armor? The potions and gold?" Red continued without acknowledging Hunter's suggestion.

"It's actually all yours," Gil confessed. "But I was going to give it back, I swear! I'm so sorry, about the griefing and the lying. I promise I won't do it again."

"*Never* trust a griefer," Hunter said and raised his sword.

"Hunter!" Roxy stepped in. "No matter what he's done in the past, Gil is our *friend*. He helped us when we were trapped in the lava."

"And he helped save Allie," added Chase.

"Without Gil, we would have never gone to the Nether and met all of you in the first place," Red agreed. "Even if he was the reason we had to."

Gil couldn't believe it. He thought that after his identity was revealed, his friends would never want to see him again, except maybe his cat Buddy. And yet, here they were, standing up on his behalf!

Hunter gawked. "What is wrong with you guys? You're defending a griefer while being trapped by griefers!"

"Not everyone is the same," Allie told him. "Gil never did anything to hurt us. And he won't, right Gil?"

"Of course not!" Gil assured them. "I swear! You're my first and only friends. I'll do anything for it to stay that way."

Hunter hesitated and then finally put down his sword.

"It doesn't mean I trust you," he warned Gil. "I'll be watching you."

Gil nodded with relief.

"Is it ok if we still call you Gil?" asked Roxy. "Glitcher is kind of...uh...griefer-y."

Gil smiled and said yes.

"Well, now that we got all this sorted out, let's find a way out of here," suggested Red. The others agreed and started to look for anything that could help them.

"How were they even able to do this?" wondered Chase. "I thought bedrock was impossible to get."

"They must be hackers messing around with different mods," theorized Red. "They can do things regular people like us can't."

"Isn't that dangerous?" asked Allie. "Can't it render everything unplayable?"

"Yes," answered Gil. "Changing the code can cause serious issues. Believe me, I know."

"It's cheating, plain and simple. They should be banned," Hunter said. "Wait a second," he added, "Gil, if you're the all-powerful Glitcher, can't you just change this bedrock into something else?"

Gil shook his head no.

"I can only access the root code from my house. I discovered a back door into the system there some time ago, and I've been using it to play around."

"Is it true?" asked Roxy. "Did you really crash the word one day?"

"If it was, we wouldn't be here, would we?" Gil responded bitterly. "Don't believe everything you hear," he directed at Hunter, who pretended not to hear him.

"Aha!" Red exclaimed. "I think I found our way out!"

The group huddled around him and saw what he was talking about. The blocks under their beds weren't bedrock. The griefers must not have wanted to disturb them while they slept and didn't think they would notice. Red mined the blocks, hoping to make a tunnel, but there was still bedrock on the sides, and the deeper he went the more worried he got. His caution paid off – the next block led straight into lava!

Everyone groaned with disappointment but didn't give up. They mined under their own beds and came to the same problem. It was bedrock or lava.

"Aw man, I thought we had it for a moment," Hunter said.

Chase sighed. "I guess we'll just have to hand over our stuff and hope they do let us out."

Suddenly, Gil got an idea.

"Here," he said, handing over his diamond armor, weapons, and all the other items in his inventory to Red. "They're yours anyway. Take them."

"This isn't a good time," Red told him. "Don't worry about it for now."

"I mean it," Gil insisted. "I *need* you to take them."

Giving in, Red picked up the items. "What are you thinking?" he asked, wondering what Gil's plan was.

"Well," Gil began, "Hunter is right. If anyone can get us out of here, it's me."

"But you said you can't do it unless you get back to your house," said Allie.

"That's right," he confirmed. "That's why I'm going home."

Red quickly grasped what Gil was going to do.

"No," he told his friend. "We'll figure out another way."

"There is no other way," said Gil, "and we can't trust those griefers to set us free, either. The Tutorial is completed so my spawn should be back at my house. From there, I'll be able to save everyone and take care of the griefers too."

Gil picked up Buddy and handed him to Red.

"Take care of Buddy for me," he said.

Red went to grab for Gil but it was too late. Gil jumped into one of the holes they dug and disappeared into the lava.

# CHAPTER 15: THE GRIEFERS' END

Shocked by Gil's heroic act, the group sat in silence and waited for any sign of their friend.

"I can't believe he sacrificed himself to save us," Hunter finally whispered with awe. "Maybe I was wrong about him."

"Sometimes people can surprise you," Red said. He was glad to have the items he worked so hard for back, but he would give them all away to see his friend again.

Roxy pointed at one of the walls. "Look!" The black and white bedrock blurred and speckles of brown began to appear. It was transforming! Soon, the entire bedrock prison was nothing more than blocks of dirt.

"He did it!" Allie cheered. She and Roxy hugged with joy.

"I have to say, he earned *my* respect," said Hunter, and Chase nodded in agreement.

Red used his trusty diamond pickaxe to clear the dirt from the exit. They were finally free! The group was just about to leave when –

"Where do you think *you're* going?" said an unmistakable voice. The griefers were back! They blocked the hallway that led outside. Their enchanted armor and weapons gleamed in the sunlight.

"We're leaving," said Red, "and there's nothing you can do to stop us."

The griefers laughed and raised their swords.

"Oh, we'll see about that," one of them cackled and sprinted towards Red. He swung the weapon but Red expertly dodged the blow. The other griefer leapt at him. Hunter came to the rescue and their swords collided with a ring. Red hit his opponent with a powerful strike. The enchanted armor seemed to take no damage! Hunter too landed several blows, and yet the griefers were unaffected. It was a losing battle! But then…

Out of nowhere, one of the griefers cried out in surprise!

"Wha…what's going on?" He fumbled, staring at his sword – or at least what used to be his sword. Now he was holding a stinky slimy squirming fish!

"Eeew!" the other griefer joined him, dropping the fish that appeared in his hand on the ground. "Gross!"

Roxy and Allie giggled at the silliness. It was definitely Gil's work! Buddy gobbled up the fish and meowed happily at the confused griefers.

"It's the Glitcher! He's doing this!" one of the griefers realized.

"I thought you said he was powerless here!" his partner argued.

"Well apparently not! He's messing with our mods!"

The second griefer began to look nervous. "What do we do?"

"We have to make the most powerful weapons of all time," the first one said. "Even the Glitcher won't be able to touch them!"

They each took out another diamond sword and began to enchant. Hunter and Red watched as the swords glowed and changed colors, over and over again. They shined brighter and brighter, until the purple light was so strong, it radiated power! But the griefers weren't done yet. They continued to add levels, high above what was normally the maximum allowed.

And then...BOOM!

Light exploded throughout the castle! Everyone covered their eyes and waited until it was safe to open them again. Red was the first to look around, followed by Hunter and the rest of the gang. The place where the griefers were looked untouched – and completely empty.

"Where did they go?" Chase wondered.

"I have no idea," answered Red.

"Well good riddance!" said Hunter. "Let's get out of here!"

"I thought you wanted to explore the castle and collect its treasures?" Red asked.

"I think I'm done with adventuring for a while," Hunter admitted. "I just want to go home, kick back, and relax."

"Me too," said Allie.

"Me three," added Roxy.

Red smiled. He was ready to go home too. Except there was one thing left to do. He needed to return Buddy to his rightful owner. But where did Gil live?

As if reading his mind, a wooden sign appeared in front of him. On it were directions to a certain village in a nearby forest biome. Red memorized the map and headed out, accompanied by the rest of the gang. He told them they didn't have to come, but they felt like they needed to thank Gil for his part in saving them and defeating the griefers. Red was happy for the company.

They walked back across the stone bridge and down to the river. A chest with boats was on the left, and fishing poles on the right. They climbed in the boats and steered in the direction of Gil's home. It was only a matter of time before they would see their friend again.

# CHAPTER 16: A SUPER WELCOME

"Y ou found me!" Gil exclaimed when he saw his friends walking towards his house. Buddy ran to him and Gil gave his kitty a great big hug.

"Of course we did," said Red. "We had to take Buddy home."

"*And* we wanted to thank you," added Roxy. "For everything."

Gil smiled and invited everyone inside. However, his house was so small the amount of people made it feel really crowded.

"You know," said Hunter, "now that you have friends, you're going to need a bigger house. In case we ever want to visit."

"I'll take care of it," Gil assured them, but Hunter put up his hands.

"Nope," he said. "It's on us. Consider it our thank you gift."

"That's a great idea!" Allie agreed.

They spent the rest of the day mining for materials and building additions to the house. Now it had a large living room area and an upstairs with extra bedrooms so his friends could spend the night. Gil could not be happier. He went to the local farmer and bought some cakes for everyone. After a day of hard work, dinner was just what they needed. They sat around the dining table and Gil brought out the treats.

"Cake? I love cake!" squealed Allie.

"Mmmm delicious," said Red. "Thanks, Gil."

"Grblt," Hunter added, his mouth full. Everyone laughed.

"So tell me something, Gil," said Roxy, "what did you do to those griefers?"

The others nodded in agreement, also wanting to know.

"Honestly, I didn't do anything," Gil confessed.

"Then what happened to them?" asked Chase.

"It's simple," Gil answered. "They overloaded. There's a reason for having a maximum enchanting level. When power gets too high, it overloads the system and – poof!" He made an explosion gesture with his hands.

"But...where did they go?" Allie asked.

"My guess is they were completely reset in a brand new generated world. One where they can't grief anyone because there's no one there."

"Nice," Hunter said, satisfied. "That'll teach 'em."

"I hope so," Gil agreed.

"What are you planning to do now?" Red asked Gil.

Gil thought about the question. He never really considered what he would be doing now that he wasn't griefing anymore. He remembered all their adventures and how hard the other griefers made their lives. An idea came to him and he smiled.

"I'm going to use my glitching powers to save people from griefers," he decided.

"Really? Like a superhero?" asked Roxy.

"Sure," said Gil. "It's better to help people than prank them. There's plenty of griefers out there, and if I can stop them from hurting others, the world would be a much better place."

"And we'll help spread the word, right guys?" Hunter offered. The others nodded enthusiastically.

"Thanks everyone," Gil said. "I couldn't ask for better friends."

That evening before going to sleep they sat by the fireplace and told stories about their past adventures. Red described a time when he saved an entire village in the plains from a zombie invasion when the wall was blown up by a creeper. Roxy and Allie told a tale of when Hunter stepped on a pressure plate inside a desert temple and almost blew everyone up! Luckily, Chase saw the TNT and snuffed out the charge first. But Gil's story was the best one yet – it was a story about a griefer who made friends and changed his ways. Everyone liked his because they knew exactly who he was talking about. The gang fell asleep that night and dreamed of friends, adventures, and treasure.

In the morning, before everyone went their own separate ways, Gil noticed a sign outside his house. It read "Gil: The Anti-Griefer".

"I love it!" Gil told his friends. They hugged goodbye and promised to see each other again soon. Gil waved as he watched his friends go, and he knew his life would never be the same.

The End

Made in the USA
San Bernardino, CA
28 July 2016